This book belongs to

RAYLA

# Show

## with Sophia

# Time

## Grace and Rosie

BY **SOPHIA GRACE BROWNLEE** AND **ROSIE McCLELLAND**

AS TOLD TO **WILLA GRACE**

ILLUSTRATED BY **SHELAGH McNICHOLAS**

ORCHARD BOOKS / NEW YORK / AN IMPRINT OF SCHOLASTIC INC.

"Look, Rosie, look!" Sophia Grace cried.
"A talent show! Let's sign up. It will be so good!"

"Oh, brother!" Rosie exclaimed. "What are we going to sing?"

Sophia Grace stopped dead in her tracks and said, "I don't know!"

They turned on their sparkly sneakers, and they headed home.

For the rest of the week, the cousins spent every afternoon . . .

. . . and every evening trying to find the PERFECT song to sing.

*Then one night . . .*

"Rosie, are you there? Come in, Rosie!" Sophia Grace said into her purple walkie-talkie radio.

"Cousin to cousin!" whispered Rosie.

"I know what song we will sing!" Sophia Grace belted out.

Then she sang a verse.

"It's purr-fect!" Rosie giggled. "So good!"

The next day, Sophia Grace and Rosie met with Ms. Plimpton, the principal, and discussed their song!

"This is going to be so grrrr-eat!" Rosie hollered.

"Furr-ocious," giggled Sophia Grace.

The two cousins practiced day and night for their performance.

They tried on different outfits and finally picked the perfect purple tutus.

"Everyone will love these," said Rosie.

"And our amazing, super-de-dooper, ginormous showstopper!" said Sophia Grace.

"And I'm sure they'll cheer for an encore," Rosie added.

"We're going to have more fun than anyone else."

Just then, Sophia Grace got a twinkle in her eye.

"Why should we have all the fun?" she said with a smile.

*The next morning at school . . .*

Sophia Grace met with her classmates and went over their BIG surprise.

"Pinkie swear!" said Sophia Grace. "It's a secret!"

And Rosie met with her classmates and did the same.

At lunchtime, Sophia Grace whispered to Rosie, "Did you know that Johnny was not going to enter the talent show because he didn't think he was good enough?"

Rosie giggled. "Our surprise will fix that."

Finally, the day of the talent show arrived.
The auditorium was packed, and excitement
was in the air. The lights dimmed,
and it was Show Time!

The Magic Society Presents
the McGoon Twins!

The Amazing Moves by Mindy!

Laugh It Up with Timothy!

The Spinning Tops
with Jack and Cameron!

Katie and Samantha,
the Hula-Hoopers!

There was a lot of commotion behind the stage.

Something BIG was happening!

"And now, ladies and gentlemen," Ms. Plimpton announced, "the last act of the evening, Show Time with Sophia Grace and Rosie."

The girls' sparkly costumes shimmered in the shining spotlight and twirled as they danced.

Sophia Grace and Rosie belted out the song.
*"Because we are all lions,
and you're gonna hear us ROAR!"*

All of a sudden, ten fierce cats pounced across the stage.

The cousins continued to sing.
*"Because we are all eagles,*
*and you're gonna see us SOAR!"*

And ten winged birds swooped across the stage.

*"Because we are all champions
and much, much MORE!"*

And the rest of Sophia Grace's and Rosie's classmates marched across the stage, each dressed like a different animal.

The audience went crazy. Everyone was on their feet!

Ms. Plimpton came onstage and announced the winner of the talent show was EVERYONE!

She leaned over and whispered to Sophia Grace and Rosie, "You two are very special. You made everyone a star!"

Sophia Grace and Rosie high-fived each other — it was the best show ever!

## From Sophia Grace:

I would like to say a very special thank you to the person who has changed our lives forever and made

our dreams come true, Auntie Ellen DeGeneres. A big thank you to Kara Hogan Leonardo.

I would like to say a big sparkly thank you to all the wonderful fans for their continued support

and send hugs and kisses to all my family.

A very special thank you to my mummy, Carly, and daddy, Dominic, for coming along on this magical journey.

Thank you to my best friend and cousin, Rosie.

## From Rosie:

I would like to say the biggest thank you to a very special lady whom I now call Auntie Ellen,

Ellen DeGeneres — and Kara Hogan Leonardo at *The Ellen DeGeneres Show*. I love you dearly.

I would like to say the fluffiest thank you with the sparkliest glitter on top to the best fans in the world.

I would also like to thank my most wonderful family, Mummy Danielle and Daddy Greg. This magical journey

I am on with my best friend and cousin, Sophia Grace, could never have been what it is without you!

Thank you. Love you always and forever!

For my dad. I will love you forever. —S.M.